Book 1 Detective Jon And The Missing Jewels

Detective Jon The All 3 Books In 1 Collection Small Book Edition

Detective Jon

Isaiah Fransen

Published by Isaiah Fransen, 2022.

This is a work of fiction. Similarities to real people, places, or events are entirely coincidental.

DETECTIVE JON THE ALL 3 BOOKS IN 1 COLLECTION SMALL BOOK EDITION

First edition. October 22, 2022.

Copyright © 2022 Isaiah Fransen.

ISBN: 979-8215389720

Written by Isaiah Fransen.

Dedication "Book Cover Design by ebooklaunch.com"

Chapter **1** <u>the party and the big heist</u>

One day there was a lady named Sally who lived in a big mansion in the middle of nowhere. She was very rich and had jewels around her neck that were more valuable than all her money as they were passed down from family to family for generations. She was having a huge party, inviting a bunch people, some she didn't even know. She also had a butler named Reggie who was helping her send out the invitations. Soon the day had come and people from all over the place were showing up to her house in the middle of nowhere. There were refreshments and lots of food. Finally Sally came out to the party and said "welcome to the party, we are going to have such a good time. There be will cake later on, followed by a huge dance. " Everyone was very excited ! Later on she met someone who was crying. Her name was Lisa and apparently she fell down and scratched her knee. Fortunately she had her butler Reggie put a bandage on it. Lisa was very grateful and said "thank you." All of a sudden someone came to the door and started knocking and Sally was surprised to see a man with what appeared to be a detective hat and coat. He said "have you seen a figure with a scarf and black coat and sunglasses?" She said "no I haven't." "Do you mind if I take a look around your mansion?" He asked. "Sure no problem" she said. Later on the cake was finally ready and everyone loved it. Then all of a sudden music started playing and everyone loved dancing to it. Then Sally saw her next door neighbor Austin. He had lots of stories to tell, including one about his dog and how he keeps escaping from his leash every time he takes him for a walk. She laughed. All of sudden power shut off all over the mansion and everyone was panicking! Suddenly Sally was pushed over and felt a tug on her neck! Immediately the lights came back on and Sally and everyone else were shocked that her jewels were gone! Then Reggie the butler told everyone there to leave immediately! However, some of the people did stay behind, including Lisa and Austin, to help find the thief and the missing jewels. All of a sudden the guy who had come earlier that evening and looked like a detective entered the room and said "I'm sorry, I don't think we were properly introduced, my name is detective Jon and I see your jewels are missing. "Don't worry, I am on the case." Sally was so grateful and said, "oh my gosh, thank you, you don't know how much those jewels mean to me!" "You can search the entire mansion, but please get my jewels back." Detective Jon said "don't worry, I won't leave until this case is solved!"

Chapter 2 <u>the mystery begins</u>

Everyone went to the living room, and detective Jon explained that he was following a strange figure in the fog on the way to the mansion. He said the reason he came was because there were reports that someone was planning to steal the jewels from Sally, but he had no clue who. Then detective Jon got out his magnifying glass and started looking around the living room for clues. He believed that the thief was still in the mansion somewhere and had not had the chance to get away with the jewels. All of a sudden he noticed something very interesting ! It seemed he found a piece of a green hedge in the living room, right by the book shelf ! "That is really odd" he said. All of sudden a book fell off the shelf, the bookshelf swung open, and a secret passage way was revealed ! "So that is how he is able to get around" detective Jon said. "There are probably a ton of secret passage ways all over the mansion" detective Jon said. "I will need a brave volunteer to go with me for back up". Lisa volunteered to go with him, so they went into the secret passage and it was very dark. Detective Jon said "watch where you step." Lisa felt something on her foot and detective Jon turned on his flashlight. It was a mouse! Lisa "said get it off! get it off !" Detective Jon kicked the mouse away, and they kept walking down the dark passage. The passage led outside and all of sudden they found themselves in the middle of a huge green hedge maze. It was really foggy and bang, the door closed behind them! Lisa said "oh great, now how are we going get out of this maze?" Detective Jon said," nothing is to tough for me to figure out." So they started walking to look for a way out. Lisa said "let's go this way", and they did, but it led to a dead end. Detective Jon said "let's go this way", but it led to another dead end. All of sudden they saw a bright light coming down a path in the hedge maze. It was Sally and Reggie the butler. They said "follow us, we will show you the way out". So eventually they got out of the hedge maze, and were going to head back to the mansion, when Reggie the butler said "I have to go do something". They said "okay", but Lisa thought something was off about Reggie the butler, so she decided to follow him. Detective Jon and Sally headed back to the mansion but when they got back to living room the thief was there dressed in a scarf, black coat and sunglasses! Suddenly the whole mansion went dark again and detective Jon heard a loud scream! When the lights came back on Sally was missing! She had been kidnapped ! Just then Austin entered the room and asked "where is Sally"? Reggie the butler and Lisa returned shortly after and they also wondered what had happened to Sally. Detective Jon said she was kidnapped and everyone said "that's terrible we need to find her and the missing jewels fast !"

Chapter 3 <u>the search for sally and the missing jewels</u>

Everyone was looking for Sally and the missing jewels all over the mansion. Detective Jon and Reggie the butler were looking upstairs. "So far nothing" said detective Jon. However they came to a room, opened the door and looked inside. "It looks like an art studio" Reggie the butler said. "This is where Sally does all her artwork I guess." Detective Jon said "I didn't know she was an artist." Then detective Jon saw there was a trail of paint on the ground that looked like foot prints. To their surprise the foot prints came up to a wall and stopped. Reggie the butler took a painting off the wall and it opened another secret passage way! It was a lot lighter than the other one they found before. Suddenly detective Jon noticed something! Apparently the light in the ceiling was a smart bulb! Then he looked around and all the lights in mansion were smart bulbs! It looked like the thief replaced all the old light bulbs around the mansion with smart bulbs. "I bet this is how he was able to shut off all the lights" said detective Jon. They quickly went into to the secret passage. Meanwhile Lisa and Austin were looking for Sally up in the attic. Suddenly Lisa heard mumbling ! She quickly looked and saw a white sheet that was moving! It turned out be Sally she was tied up and had a white cloth over her mouth. They quickly untied her. She said "thank you for saving me!" Lisa said "what happened" and Sally said "I don't know, the last thing I remember the room went black and I was knocked out, and then I woke up here in the attic all tied up!" Lisa and Austin were both glad she was safe. Austin had to go back home to feed his dog but said he would be right back. Lisa and Sally said "okay see you when you get back" and quickly they both headed back to the living room for a nice cup of tea. Meanwhile detective Jon and Reggie the butler were looking in the secret passage way, when all of a sudden, the lights turned off again! Reggie the butler was scared of the dark so he headed back and detective Jon was all by himself but he kept moving along the secret passage way.

Chapter 4 <u>the secret room</u>

Detective Jon kept moving down the secret passage way and saw a light at the end of the passage way. The light was shining through a door to another secret room, he opened the door and sure enough, there was the thief with the scarf, black coat, and sunglasses. He was trying to open up a huge safe in the secret room with jewels that he has stolen. Somehow those jewels must be a key? All of a sudden, the thief spotted detective Jon and rushed out the door quickly. Detective Jon went after him but he was very fast and quickly went out the passage way into the art studio. The thief made his way downstairs. Meanwhile, Sally and Lisa were having tea in the living room when the thief ran into the living room and Sally and Lisa screamed. Detective Jon ran into the living room and the thief scampered out the secret passage they took before and got away again. Detective Jon, Lisa, and Sally quickly took after the thief down the secret passage way out to the hedge maze. They soon got to the hedge maze and it was even more foggy than before and the door slammed closed behind them again. Then they heard foot steps and all of a sudden there was a strange figure ahead of them. They followed him, but lost him in the maze. They ended up going deeper into the hedge maze and eventually they were trapped. The figure all of sudden appeared again and they chased him again even deeper into the hedge maze. Finally they caught him, however, it was not the thief. To their surprise it was Sally's landscaper Kevin. Sally asked "what are you doing here so late at night" then Kevin said "I was doing some watering of the garden but then it got really foggy and I got lost". So now all four of them were trapped and had to find a way out, but detective Jon said he would try his hardest to make sure they got out safely.

Chapter 5 <u>finding a way out</u>

Detective Jon and everyone were still trying to find a way out of the hedge maze. They went one way and ended up at a dead end and then went the other way and still ended up at a dead end. The situation seemed hopeless Then detective Jon heard a sound and told everyone to follow that noise. And so they did. They finally got out of hedge maze! They discovered the noise was Sally's chef Chris banging pots and pans together. He said "I saw you guys were trapped in the hedge maze from one of the windows of the mansion and thought I would help get you out" Sally and detective Jon and everyone were so grateful and thanked Chris for saving the day. They all went back to the house but when they tried to open the door it was locked! Then they tried to open the other door and it was locked as well! It looked like the thief locked all the doors to the mansion! Sally cried "oh no, now what"? Detective Jon said "we will find another way in". So detective Jon found a big ladder and he said "the only way in is to climb up to the roof and go thorough one of the upstairs windows". Everyone was like, are you crazy? Detective Jon said "it's the only way". Everyone went up the ladder one at a time, really slowly. All of them made it to the roof. Sally said "okay this great detective Jon, now how do we get into the window"? Detective Jon said "we hang upside down, open the window and push ourselves in" Everyone was like "your kidding me right" "That is even more crazy!" Detective Jon quickly hung upside down from the roof, opened up the window, and pushed himself in. Everyone else went cautiously in one at a time and everyone made it safely but they were really not happy with detective Jon."

That was really dangerous detective Jon" said Sally. Detective Jon said "okay I promise we won't do that again" Finally they all went back downstairs and Chris the chef went back to the kitchen. When they all got back downstairs, they noticed that Reggie the butler had disappeared. Everyone shouted "we have to find him"! Detective Jon said "don't worry we wil!l"

Chapter 6 <u>the search for reggie the butler</u>

Everyone was looking all over for Reggie the butler. Sally and Lisa were looking in the attic and found nothing there, detective Jon and Kevin the landscaper were looking in the dining room and found no sign of him. Then detective Jon remembered something. "I found a secret room in a secret passage in the art studio" he said. Kevin the landscaper said "really, let's go check there then." So they went into the art studio and into the secret passage to go to the secret room. When they got there the door was locked but all of a sudden they found another room close by. They went into the room and it looked like a supply closet. They saw all the old light bulbs that were replaced with the smart bulbs. Suddenly they heard a mumbling and sure enough there was Reggie the butler all tied up with ropes and a gag in his mouth. They quickly untied him and he said "the thief brought me here." Then all of sudden the door to the other room opened. It was the thief, and he was getting away with what looked to be a bag of gold! They chased him, but all of a sudden the lights went out again and he got away. They went back into the room where the thief was and saw that the safe has been opened and whatever was in it was gone! Detective Jon found a clue, a piece of lettuce on the floor. Then detective Jon thought of something," I think our thief is Chris the chef." Just then Austin came back from feeding his dog and said, "what did I miss"? Detective Jon said "it's time to catch ourselves a chef." They met everyone downstairs and planned to set a trap for the chef. They all went to the dining room and waited for Chris the chef to bring dinner to Sally. Suddenly Chris the chef walks into the dining room and they threw a net on top of him. Chris the chef said "what is the meaning of this", but all of a sudden the jewels fell out of his pocket. He shouted "how did those get there?" Detective Jon said "no excuses, you stole the jewels and the gold, and now I'm phoning the police". Sally was really disappointed, "how could you do this Chris?" The police came and took Chris the chef away but something still did not feel right to detective Jon. But Sally said everything was fine, and everyone quickly thanked detective Jon for all his help. Then he left and everyone said goodbye. Detective Jon was walking back home when all of sudden he thought of something! Chris the chef was with us when we were locked outside, so he couldn't have been the thief as the thief was inside the house! And he was like, oh no! And he quickly went back to the mansion but everyone had disappeared!

Chapter 7 <u>finding everyone and the real thief</u>

Detective Jon went to the police station and told the police that there was a terrible mistake and they released Chris the chef and he was wondering what was going on? Detective Jon said the real thief was still at large and that he had kidnapped everyone at the mansion. Chris the chef was shocked and said "we have to find them and the real thief!" They headed back to the mansion. Detective Jon said "first we have to find Sally." They looked everywhere. First the dining room and then the living room and could not find her. Then they went upstairs to the art studio and into the secret passage where they went to the secret room. There they found Sally in the safe, all tied up and with a sheet on her mouth. They untied her and they asked "are you alright?" Sally said "yes, but where are the others?" Then they heard a mumble coming from the supply closest. Sure enough it was Lisa, all tied up with sheet over her mouth! They asked again "are you alright?" Lisa said "yes" Then they went up to the attic and found Reggie the butler tied up and with a sheet over his mouth! They untied him and once again they said "are you alright?" and he said "yes." Then they went downstairs to the secret passage in the living room and out to the hedge maze. They found Kevin the landscaper all tied up and with a sheet over his mouth. They untied him and once again said, "are you all right?" and he said "yes". Then detective Jon realized it was a trap! Sure enough the thief threw a huge net over top of them! Then he took off his scarf and sunglasses and revealed himself to be none other than Austin, Sally's next door neighbor!

Chapter 8 <u>Going after Austin through the hedge maze</u>

Austin turned out to be the real thief. Everyone was shocked and asked "why would you do this Austin?" He said "because I wanted the jewels and the gold, so I could be rich like Sally!" "I out smarted detective Jon, as he was so foolish to blame Chris the chef instead of me! I put the lettuce down on the floor to make detective Jon think it was Chris the chef, I also put the jewels in the Chris the chef's coat while he was not wearing it. Then once you left, I kidnapped everyone and took the jewels back!" Detective Jon said "you won't get away with this Austin!" All of a sudden, detective Jon broke free from the net! Austin started to run and make his get away! Detective Jon freed everyone else and said "after him!" They quickly started taking multiple directions through the hedge maze trying to catch Austin. Austin made his way out of the hedge maze on the other side, and took off in a van with the gold and the jewels. He was headed to the airport to make his way out of the country. Everyone else made it out of the hedge maze on the other side just in time to see the van taking off! "It looks like he's heading to the airport" sally said. "We have to stop him!" detective Jon said, but they had no transportation! Luckily Kevin the landscaper had and extra van and he said "hop in!" Detective Jon said "let's catch us a thief!"

Chapter 9 <u>the airport</u>

Detective Jon and everyone were following Austin to the airport. Suddenly they were there and Austin ran out of the van and into the airport. Detective Jon said "after him!" They quickly ran into the airport where there were thousands of people. Sally shouted "great, how are we supposed to find him now!" Detective Jon said "we will find a way!" There was someone eating at the restaurant in the airport and they went and asked the guy "have you seen a guy in a black coat?" and he said "yes, I just saw him sneaking past security." Detective Jon said "thank you for the information!" They went and told the security guards there was a thief on the loose and they let them past the security gate. There was Austin getting ready to board the plan! Detective Jon yelled "found you Austin!" Austin started to run off again! Sally said" we've got to get him." Detective Jon said "I already took care of that!" All of a sudden Chris the chef sneaked behind Austin and threw a net over top of him! He shouted "NO!" Detective Jon took the jewels and the gold from him and gave it back to Sally and called the police. The police took Austin away and then Sally had another announcement to make She was going to have another party and everyone was invited including detective Jon!

Chapter 10 <u>the celebration</u>

Sally organized a party to celebrate getting her jewels and gold back. Everyone was having an awesome time. There was a huge band playing and cake and lots of food! All of a sudden Sally came out and thanked everyone including detective Jon for getting her jewels and her gold back. Just then detective Jon got a phone call saying that he was needed at the history museum. Detective Jon thanked everyone for helping with the case and for the party and all the food and then left. Meanwhile Lisa and Sally were wondering why detective Jon was needed at the history museum. They turned on the TV and it turned out a rare artifact was stolen from the museum. Sally was like "I hope he going to be alright?" Lisa said "I'm sure he going to be just fine!"

Book 2 Detective Jon AND THE MISSING ARTIFACT

Chapter 1 The Museum and the Missing Artifact

Detective Jon was on his way to the museum where an artifact had been stolen. When he got there, the museum manager, Megan, came up to him and said "an artifact from the museum has been stolen !" Detective Jon said "don't worry, I will find it!" The museum manager Megan said "you will help?" "Great!" "The missing artifact is a Viking helmet which belonged to a brave warrior who lived years and years ago." Detective Jon said "don't worry, I'm on the case!" Just then Joe the janitor came up to detective Jon and said "I didn't see anyone last night who could have stolen the artifact, but I'll help you by keeping an eye out." Detective Jon said "OK thanks." Then detective Jon went to the museum gift shop. The gift shop cashier was named Ben and he said "you're welcome to look around." So detective Jon went and looked around and found something very interesting! It looked like footprints and they went behind a wall. He pulled some of the items off a shelf and found a secret passage! It looked like it went underground! It was very creepy! The gift shop cashier Ben said "how did I not notice that before?" Detective Jon said "OK I will find out where this leads!" He went down The secret passage to see where it went. It went to an old exhibit. It looked like no one had been down there for years. However Detective Jon noticed that there was an old Viking ship exhibit along with some Viking armor. Just then he saw what looked like a moving Viking, and he realized that's our thief! He quickly chased him down the hallways of the old exhibit, but then he was gone! Then detective Jon went back upstairs to tell Megan the museum manager what he had discovered. "There is a guy dressed as a Viking on the loose and he's wearing the Viking helmet that he stole!" Just then the lights went out, and the guy who dressed as a Viking appeared and said "leave this museum right now detective Jon, or I will have to take drastic measures!" Then he disappeared! Megan the museum manager said "what am I going to do, if that Viking appears he will scare everyone away and I will have to close the museum!" Detective Jon said "he doesn't scare me that easily, don't worry, I will not leave until this case is solved!"

Chapter 2 Searching for Clues and the Thief

Detective Jon went to look for clues and the thief. Then he noticed something that looked to be a red scarf. "I wonder who this belongs to?" he said, and he picked it up and took it with him. Then he went outside to the back of the museum where there was a garden that had old statues. He saw someone doing yard work in the garden. The gardener's name was Dan. Detective Jon said "do you know who this scarf belongs to?" Dan said "no". Then detective Jon saw someone at the other end of the garden. It turned out to be the thief dressed as a Viking! The Viking quickly said "you have been warned, now I will take my first victim!" Immediately Dan the gardener disappeared! Detective Jon was In shock! How in the world did they just disappear? Quickly detective Jon went back to Megan the museum manager and they went into the office. Detective Jon told Megan the museum manager how Dan the gardener just disappeared. She said "no way, how could that happen?" "Don't worry I will find him", Detective Jon said, "But I have a question, do you know how old the museum is?" She said "at least 100 years old?". Detective Jon said "wow, that's really old, I'm wondering if there's traps in this museum that the thief might have used to make it look like Dan the gardener magically disappeared?" Just then a woman walked in the door. She turned out to be a fashion designer named Alice. She said "have you seen my scarf?" Detective Jon said "I found this scarf on the floor, is it yours?" She said "yes"! Then all of a sudden the lights went out again, and the thief, dressed as a Viking came in and said "you have been warned to leave, now I will take my second victim!" All of a sudden detective Jon heard a scream and the lights came back on! Megan the museum manager was gone! Then Detective Jon heard people panicking! He went outside the office and there was the thief dressed as a Viking terrorizing the museum! Everyone at the museum was heading out the door. Joe the janitor was telling everyone not to panic. So was Alice the fashion designer, but it was too late. Everyone left and the museum was empty. Detective Jon said "if we don't do something fast the museum will have to close, and the Thief will get away!" Joe the janitor And Alice the fashion designer said to detective Jon "don't worry we have your back!" Detective Jon said "thanks you guys!" "Now we have to find Dan the gardener and Megan the museum manager quickly!" "Everyone follow me!" And they quickly went to the gift shop. Ben The gift shop cashier was nowhere to be seen. Alice the fashion designer said "do you think the thief dressed as a Viking got him too?" And detective Jon said "we will find out!" They quickly went down the secret passage in hopes of finding Dan the gardener, Megan the museum manager And Ben the gift shop cashier.

Chapter 3 The Search for the Missing People

Detective Jon, Joe the janitor and Alice the fashion designer came out of the secret passage Into the old exhibit. It was really dark, and Alice the fashion designer was afraid of the dark. Joe the janitor said "don't worry I'll hold your hand." Quickly detective Jon noticed something. There was a support beam that was missing from the old exhibit and he said "be careful everyone, do not make a sound or otherwise the part of the exhibit we're in could collapse!" So they carefully tiptoed through that part of the exhibit. All of a sudden Joe the janitor sneezed, and the whole part of the exhibit started to collapse! Detective Jon said "run as fast as you can!" They were running for their lives and just made it to the other side of the exhibit! But now they had no way out! So they quickly kept going to find another way out and then they stumbled upon what looked like an old huge safe. It looked like it had been opened. They went into the safe and found what appeared to be an old mine shaft! They quickly went inside and saw someone had been digging for something. They looked around the mine and found piles of gold! Then detective Jon realized that both cases, the one he solved with the missing jewels, and this one were connected! Detective Jon said "I have to get back to Sally's mansion fast!" "We have to find a way out of here" said Joe the janitor. Then they saw a mine cart and they hopped in. "I don't know where this goes," said detective Jon, "but hold on!" They quickly rode the mine cart through the mine and to the other side where there was a flash of daylight. They came out of the mine, but then detective Jon saw that they were in the middle of nowhere! It did not seem far from where Sally's mansion was however, so they quickly started to head towards Sally's mansion.

Chapter 4 Return to Sally's Mansion

Detective Jon And everyone made it to Sally's mansion. They went and knocked on the door. Sally opened the door and said "Detective Jon, what are you doing here, and who are these people?" So they introduced themselves."Hi my name is Joe the janitor at the museum", and "my name is Alice, I'm a fashion designer." Sally said "nice to meet you both, come inside". Once they got inside detective Jon explained to Sally that both cases, the one he solved with the missing jewels, and the one at the museum were both connected. Sally said "that's crazy!" So they went to the safe at Sally's mansion and looked at the gold. It was identical to the gold they found at the museum mine! All of a sudden the mansion lights went out, and the thief dressed as a Viking appeared! He said, "You have gone too far now, I shall take my third victim!" Sure enough, Joe the janitor disappeared! Alice the fashion designer said "this is terrible,now what do we do detective Jon?" "Don't worry we will find them," said detective Jon. Then they thought they had better head to the airport to look for clues. So quickly they left Sally's mansion. Sally waved goodbye and said "good luck detective Jon!" So detective Jon and Alice the fashion designer were on their way to the airport to look for clues .

Chapter 5 Return to the Airport to Search for Clues

Detective Jon and Alice the fashion designer were on the way to the airport to search for clues. They went into the airport and went to ask a security guard If they could look for clues. The security guard Said "yes,sure." And then they went outside toward the runway at the airport and detective Jon noticed a private airplane. He went to take a look and noticed crates with tarps over them. He removed the tarps from the crates and found more gold! This gold also looked identical to the ones they found at the museum And at Sally's mansion! Detective Jon said "I think I got this mystery just about figured out!" "Now we must head back to the mine!" So detective Jon and Alice the fashion designer headed back to the mine. When they got there the thief dressed as a Viking appeared! He said, "this is your final warning, now I shall take my fourth victim!" And instantly, Alice the fashion designer disappeared! Now detective Jon was all by himself. Detective Jon moved on into the mine

Chapter 6 Into the Deep Parts of the Mine

Detective Jon was heading deeper into mine when he noticed there was a cliff and at the bottom of the cliff was a snake pit full of large snakes! He had to find a way across! Then he saw a rope and he quickly lassoed the rope to the other ledge and it caught on to a rock. He quickly tied his end of the rope to another rock and started to tightrope across! Very carefully he made it to the other side. He walked further into the mine and found multiple tunnels. He didn't know which one to take. He chose the most left tunnel and carefully walked down it. It got really dark and all of sudden someone grabbed him from behind! Detective Jon managed to turn on his flashlight. It was none other than the thief dressed as a Viking! He knocked detective Jon unconscious! The thief dressed as a Viking said "you have been warned, nothing can stop me now!!

Chapter 7 Breaking Free and Getting Out of the Mine

Detective Jon woke up all tied up by ropes and all of his other friends that were kidnapped we're right beside him, all tied up by ropes as well! Detective Jon noticed something!! There was dynamite and the whole mine was about to blow up!! Everyone else screamed, "we have to get out of here, detective Jon do something!" Detective Jon tried to reach for his pocket knife but could not reach it. Alice the fashion designer tried to use a stick to reach for detective Jon's pocket knife. She eventually got it and managed to get it to detective Jon.Detective Jon quickly broke free and then freed everyone else. Detective Jon yelled, "we have to get out of here!" So they quickly started running like the wind! Then detective Jon remembered the Cliff! He yelled, "whoa, everyone stop!" Everyone saw the Cliff with the snake pit below, and said, "what now detective Jon?" He said, "we have to tightrope across" Everyone was like, "are you crazy?" "No I'm not, trust me!" So they went across, one at a time, and made it. They got outside just in time as the mine blew up! By the time it was done the mine was completely destroyed! Now everyone wondered where Ben the gift shop cashier was. Suddenly the thief that was dressed like a Viking appeared, took off the Viking helmet and revealed himself to be Ben the gift shop cashier!

Chapter 8 Ben Making His Getaway

Ben the gift shop cashier turned out to be the thief!! Everyone was like, "how could you do this?" He explained that Austin, the guy that stole the missing jewels, was his brother and they were originally partners. But Austin, the one who stole the missing jewels, decided to keep the jewels and the gold for himself,but he got caught, and now he is in jail. Now I will do what my brother couldn't, I will smuggle the gold out of the country!" Detective Jon said, "you won't get away with this!" Ben the gift shop cashier said to detective Jon, "you're wrong, I will!" Ben the gift shop cashier threw a net on top of everyone and quickly made his getaway! Detective Jon broke free and started chasing him! He chased him through the woods but then there were two different paths. He didn't know which one to go down, so you tried his luck and chose the path on the right. He went down the path and he came up to a cave. He went into the cave and heard a weird sound! It sounded like a growl,and he quickly realized it was a bear! He was like, "oh no, what am I gonna to do now!"

Chapter 9 Escaping the Bear and Finding a Way Out of the Woods

Detective Jon was face to face with a bear when all of a sudden everyone caught up with him and Megan the museum manager used a bear horn to scare the bear away! Unfortunately detective Jon was already badly hurt! Megan the museum manager said, "we have to get him to a hospital and fast" Quickly they started carrying detective Jon but they were lost in the woods! Eventually they came to a lake in the woods. There was an old deserted cabin on the lakeshore and it was getting dark. Megan the museum manager said, "looks like we're spending the night here." Everyone took turns taking care of detective Jon and in the morning they started to look for a way out of the woods. They came up to an old rickety bridge. Megan the museum manager said "I will cross carrying detective Jon, but the rest of you we'll have to cross one at a time." So Megan the museum manager crossed the bridge while carrying detective Jon, and made it safely to the other side. Then Joe the janitor started to cross the rickety old bridge and made it. Then Dan the gardener started to cross the rickety old bridge and made it. Finally Alice the fashion designer started to cross the rickety old bridge but as she got closer to the end, the rickety old bridge started to collapse! She was running towards the end of the bridge,but the rickety old bridge collapsed before she could get there! She grabbed onto a ledge and yelled "help" So everyone ran to the edge of the ledge and Megan the museum manager hung over the ledge and grabbed Alice the fashion designer's hand. Everyone started to pull Alice the fashion designer back up. She was very grateful!

"That was very close," said Alice, the fashion designer. They quickly made their way to the road and called an ambulance. The ambulance came and took detective Jon to the hospital

Chapter 10

The Hospital

Everyone was at the hospital waiting to hear if detective Jon was alright. The doctor came out of the room and said detective Jon was alright but would need some time to recover. Everyone was so happy to hear that detective Jon was alright. They all went to the cafeteria to get a cup of coffee. While they were at the cafeteria they saw someone who looked familiar. It turned out to be none other than Ben the gift shop cashier! The thief!! Ben, the gift shop cashier noticed them and quickly started to run. They took off after him! They went through the lobby and down the stairs into the parkade. When they got there they did not know where he went. Suddenly they saw a car speeding out of the parkade! It turned out to be Ben, the gift shop cashier speeding towards the airport! They went back upstairs and detective Jon was all better. They told him they saw Ben the gift shop cashier take off to the airport. Detective Jon said, "we have to stop him!" They quickly all ran to get a taxi. They told the taxi driver to get to the airport as fast as he could! They had to stop Ben, the gift shop cashier, from smuggling the artifact and the gold out of the country!

Chapter 11 Stopping Ben at all Costs

Detective Jon and everyone made it to the airport but there was a huge crowd and they couldn't see Ben, the gift shop cashier anywhere! They shouted, "move out of the way everyone," "there's a thief on the loose!" Everyone moved out of the way and when they got into the airport they gave a security guard a description of Ben the gift shop cashier and asked if he had seen this person. He said "yes and his plane is about to take off." Detective Jon asked "can we get access to the runway?" and the security guard said "yes". They quickly ran outside to the runway and found out that Ben, the gift shop cashier was about to take off! Detective Jon yelled to one of the runway security people "stop that plane!" He tried to stop it but it was too late! Ben the gift shop cashier had taken off! Detective Jon asked, "where is he heading?" He said "the United States, if you want I have a pilot that can take you there."Detective Jon and everyone said "OK!" The pilot arrived and said, ``my name is Julie, how can I be of assistance?" Detective Jon and everyone said, "that guy has just taken off to the United States." "He has stolen an artifact and gold from the museum"! The pilot Julie said "oh no, that's terrible, I can take you there no problem." They got on the plane and started to take off to the United States. Julie the pilot said, "are you all ready?" Detective Jon and everyone said "yes." "OK, here we go!"said Julie,and they went on the runway and took off.

Chapter 12 The storm

Detective Jon and everyone we're flying on their way to the United States to stop Ben the gift shop cashier from stealing the artifact and the gold from the museum. Suddenly though, detective Jon noticed clouds with rain and lightning! Then strong winds started to move the plane off course and there was heavy turbulence! Julie the pilot radioed mayday to the control tower, but no one was responding! Detective Jon and everyone we're terrified! All of a sudden, lightning struck the plane and they lost one wing! They were almost to their destination in the United states. Julie the pilot was going to try something that no pilot had done before! She was going to try to land the plane with only one wing! She shouted, "everyone hold on tight!" and she quickly started heading down to the runway. The plane reached the runway and started sliding across sideways! Luckily the plane stopped and everyone was safe! They quickly scrambled off the plane one at a time! Everyone was like, "oh, that was so close we barely made it!" Now detective Jon said, "we must find Ben the gift shop cashier right away, before he gets away!"

Chapter 13 Finding Ben in the Airport

Detective Jon and everyone were searching the airport for Ben the gift shop cashier. They quickly noticed Ben by the luggage! He spotted them and yelled, "how did you guys get here?" Julie the pilot said, "I brought them here!" Ben, the gift shop cashier, started to run towards the exit and quickly jumped into a taxi and drove away! Everyone said, "now what?" Detective Jon said, "we will have to get a taxi as quickly as we can!" They found a taxi and told the taxi driver to go after Ben! So they chased him down the road and were catching up to him! Ben the gift shop cashier said to his taxi driver, "drive faster!" The driver said "why?" Ben the gift shop cashier said "just go!" The driver quickly started to go a bit faster but detective Jon and everyone we're still catching up! Ben the gift shop cashier yelled "can't you go any faster?" Then the taxi driver knew something was going on and pulled over. Detective Jon and everyone caught up, and Ben the gift shop cashier got out of the taxi and ran into an abandoned building! Detective Jon and everyone ran into the abandoned building after him!

Chapter 14 Catching Ben in the Abandoned Building

Detective Jon and everyone we're trying to find Ben the gift shop cashier in the abandoned building! They quickly ran up the stairs and sure enough there he was! They started chasing him and he went up some more stairs and onto the roof! He had nowhere left to run. Detective Jon said "you have nowhere left to run, give it up!" Ben the gift shop cashier said, "never!" He quickly jumped over the edge of the building and started to climb down a ladder! Detective Jon was not giving up and he quickly started to climb down the ladder too! Ben the gift shop cashier got to the bottom first, and then he started shaking the ladder! He said, "this is your end detective Jon!" but then detective Jon let go of the ladder and did a backflip and got behind Ben, and put him in handcuffs! Everyone scampered down the ladder and asked, "how did you do that detective Jon?" He said "easy, gymnastics class!" Detective Jon took the artifact and gold from Ben's suitcase. The police took Ben, the gift shop cashier away. Megan the museum manager yelled at Ben, "by the way you are fired!" So Ben was gone, and detective Jon said let's go home and get these back to the museum!

Chapter 15 Returning the Items to The Museum

Detective Jon and everyone got back to the museum. They quickly put the Viking helmet, which was the stolen artifact, back on the shelf. They put the gold into Megan, the museum managers safe. Later, the next day, they reopened the old Viking exhibit that they had found behind the gift shop. Everyone was celebrating and having a blast! Detective Jon said he had better be going when, all of a sudden, a dark cloud with green lightning came crashing down into the museum!! All of a sudden a wizard appeared! Detective Jon couldn't believe it! The wizard said, "my name is Ralph the wizard, I have a mystery in another world for you detective Jon!" "This mystery is really critical, as it could mean the fate of the entire universe!" Detective Jon agreed to go with Ralph the wizard to the other world! Everyone else was "like are you crazy detective Jon?" Detective Jon said "maybe I am or maybe I ain't!" So detective Jon and Ralph the wizard went through the portal to the other world! Everyone was amazed that they were gone!!

Book 3 Detective Jon And The Hidden World

Chapter 1
Entering the Hidden
World

Detective Jon and Ralph the wizard we're heading through the portal to the other world ! Detective Jon asked Ralph the wizard "what is the other world called?" He said "it's called "The Hidden World"." He also said, "it's a lot different from the world you come from". "How different"? asked Detective Jon. Ralph the wizard said "this world is full of unicorns, trolls, warlocks, and dragons". Detective Jon said, "that sounds scary"! And then Ralph the wizard said, "we are almost to the

Hidden World!" "Hold on tight"! They landed in Ralph the Wizard's Castle! Ralph the Wizard said to detective Jon, "this way quickly"! They hurried upstairs to the top of the castle. Detective Jon looked out the window and saw that the world was a lot different from the world he came from! Ralph the Wizard told Detective Jon that there was an evil dragon named Carey and her pet crow named Doug, and they wanted to steal his magic wand and use it to take over the universe! Ralph the wizard said "they will start with your world Detective Jon, then after that, the universe!" DetectiveJon said, "That is just terrible!" "How do we stop them?" "How do we?" said Ralph the Wizard. "You have to Detective Jon!" "In order to do this you must collect 3 different element crystals from across the Hidden World. "These elements are water, fire, and Ice." "However, they are guarded by 3 different creatures." "The first element is guarded by a unicorn named Sophia." "The second element is guarded by a troll named Bentley." "The final element Is guarded by one of the most dangerous creatures of all, the Oatmeal Warlock!" "Each of them will put you to some kind of test to see if you are worthy!" All of a sudden, Doug the Crow swooped in and grabbed the wand out of Ralph the Wizard's hand! He said "finally I have the wand!" "Carey the Dragon will be quite pleased !" Ralph the wizard yelled to Detective Jon, "quick, grab the wand!" However, Doug The Crow flew away with the wand! Using the wand's power, he started to destroy the castle! Ralph the Wizard screamed to Detective Jon, "We have to get out of here before the whole castle collapses on top of us!" So they ran down the stairs and out the front door! Safely outside, Ralph the Wizard said to Detective Jon, "hurry, you must go now and get the 3 elements before Doug the crow gets the wand to Carey the dragon!" Detective Jon said "okay, I'll do my best !" And so Detective Jon started his journey through the Hidden World to collect the 3 elements and stop Carey the Dragon And Doug The Crow from taking over the universe !

Chapter 2
The First Test

Detective Jon was on his way to retrieve the first element. He came up to a forest which was very dark and spooky! Bravely He started heading into the forest. As he was walking through the forest, he suddenly heard galloping footsteps. It sounded like a horse! Detective Jon started running, and all of a sudden he came up to a lake. There was a unicorn on the other side! Detective Jon yelled, "are you Sophia The Unicorn?" She shouted back, "yes, if you can cross the lake I will give you the water element." Detective Jon looked around to find a way across the lake. All of a sudden a boat appeared! Detective Jon wondered for a moment,"how did that get here?" He hopped into the boat and started to row across the lake. However, when he got to the middle of the lake, there were crocodiles! The crocodiles were trying to eat his boat! Detective Jon yelled at Sophia the Unicorn, "You didn't say that there were crocodiles in this Lake!" Sophia the Unicorn responded, "it's part of the test Detective Jon!" Detective Jon yelled back, "are you crazy?" So Detective Jon Had to think of something fast! Then he remembered he had a sandwich in his pocket. So he quickly tossed the sandwich into the lake, and the crocodiles went after it! Then he paddle the boat across as quickly as he could, and made it to the other side! Sophia the Unicorn congratulated Detective Jon, saying, "you passed the first test!" So Sophia the Unicorn gave Detective Jon a crystal which was the water element! Detective Jon said, "thank you" to Sophia The Unicorn, and put the water element crystal in his pocket. He was about to say goodbye to Sophia the Unicorn when all of a sudden Doug The Crow appeared! He said "how is this possible? "You got the water element!" He was very angry, and he used Ralph the Wizard's magic wand to send an army of crows after both of them! Doug The Crow said, "let's see you both try to get away from my crow friends!" and Doug The Crow quickly flew off. Detective Jon and Sophia the Unicorn both started to run away from the army of crows!

Chapter 3
Escaping
The Army Of Crows

Detective Jon and Sophia the Unicorn we're trying to escape the army of crows! The path quickly came to a dead end and Detective Jon said, "what do we do now?" Sophia the Unicorn had an idea, she said, "quick Detective Jon, use the water element"! So Detective Jon pulled out the water element from his pocket,and all of a sudden it started to rain really hard! The crows flew away! Detective Jon wondered what had just happened? Sophia the Unicorn said, "that's the power of the water element! It causes rain to fall from the sky!" Detective Jon said, "That's crazy!" They continued on their way and they suddenly came up to a volcano. Sophia the Unicorn said to Detective Jon, "you must climb up the volcano, and on the top you will meet Bentley the Troll!" Detective Jon said, "okay"! So he quickly started climbing the volcano to confront Bentley the Troll.

Chapter 4
Confronting
Bentley The Troll

Detective Jon made it to the top of the volcano. All of a sudden he came up to a bridge. He started to cross the bridge when all of a sudden, out of nowhere, a troll jumped onto the bridge! Detective Jon said, "are you Bentley the troll?" The troll growled "yes and you're trespassing on my volcano!" "Now you will pay!" Detective Jon said, "well I only have a dollar!" Bentley the troll said, "I don't mean that kind of pay, I meant pay with your life!" Suddenly, Bentley the troll pulled out the fire element and It started throwing fireballs at Detective Jon! Detective Jon was like, "yikes!" He frantically tried to dodge the fireballs! All of a sudden the bridge ropes were on fire! Detective Jon Said to Bentley the troll, "you have to stop!" "you're going to Destroy us both!" Bentley the troll realized the bridge was on fire and that below the bridge was hot lava! He screamed "oh no!" They both started running to the other side of the bridge as fast as they could! Detective Jon made it. However Bentley the troll was hanging onto a ledge above the hot lava! Detective Jon realized he had to do something! So he found some rope that was still intact from the bridge and he quickly tossed the rope to Bentley the troll and started to pull him up! Bentley the troll said, "why did you save me?" Detective Jon Said "I thought it was the right thing to do!" Bentley the troll said, "as a token of my appreciation, I will give you the fire element! Detective Jon said "thanks!" However, just then, Doug The Crow saw them on top of the volcano! He swooped down and asked, "how did you escape my Army of crows?" Then Doug The Crow used Ralph the Wizard's Magic wand to make the volcano erupt! He said, "let's see you try to get away from this!" and then Doug The Crow flew away! Detective Jon was like, "what are we going to do?"

Chapter 5
Escaping The
Erupting Volcano

Detective Jon and Bentley the troll were wondering how they were going to escape the volcano In time! Just then, Sophia the Unicorn came up the volcano and said, "quick, hop on both of you!" So Detective Jon and Bentley the troll both hopped on Sophia the Unicorn's back and they started heading down the volcano! But the lava was catching up to them fast,and Detective Jon said, "we have to move faster somehow!" Just ahead, Bentley the troll Saw what appeared to be a jump! He said to Sophia the Unicorn, "can you make that jump to safety?"She said "hang on" and they started moving really fast! Sophia the unicorn took the jump and flew as hard as she could! They just made it to safety before the lava got to them! However, Doug The Crow was secretly watching them from a tree top as they were escaping the volcano! He said, "I have to do something or otherwise they will get the 3 elements!" "Carey the Dragon and I will be defeated!" Suddenly Doug the Crow had a brilliant and terrible idea! "I will get Rodney the Giant to catch them, and he will take them back to his castle and eat them for lunch!" so Doug the Crow headed off to Rodney the Giant's castle. Meanwhile, Detective Jon, Sophia the Unicorn, and Bentley the Troll were off to confront the Oatmeal Warlock.

Chapter 6
Confronting The
Oatmeal Warlock

Detective Jon and the others arrived at the Oatmeal Warlocks castle which was completely made of ice. They quickly went inside and once inside, Sophia the Unicorn said,"hurry, we must get to the oatmeal warlocks throne room!" They all started running to the oatmeal warlocks throne room! All of a sudden, Bentley the Troll slipped on the ice and started sliding down the long hallway! Detective Jon yelled, "we must help him!" So they carefully ran and tried to catch up to Bentley the Troll down the long,slippery hallway! They eventually caught up to him and helped him to get back up on his feet! Then they headed on their way to the throne room and finally made it to the door. They knocked on the door and the Oatmeal Warlock yelled, "who dares disturb the oatmeal warlock?" "It's us, Detective Jon, Sophia the Unicorn, and Bentley the Troll." The Oatmeal Warlock opened the door and said, "you better not try anything, or I will use my oatmeal powers against you Detective Jon!" Detective Jon said, "we are just here for the Ice element." The Oatmeal Warlock said, "if you can find a way to unfreeze this bowl of oatmeal, I will give you the ice element." Detective Jon had an idea, he used the fire element to unfreeze the bowl of oatmeal. The Oatmeal Warlock said, "you are a genius!" "I haven't had a bowl of oatmeal in ages!" "You may now take the ice element! Everyone was like great, "we have all 3 elements, now we can stop Doug the Crow and Carey the Dragon from taking over the universe!" However, out of nowhere, Ralph the

Wizard appeared and said, "we don't have much time!" "We must now get to Carey the Dragon's cave before she opens the portal to Detective Jons world!" All of a sudden a big hand came through the castle window and grabbed everyone! And Ralph the wizard was like "oh no, not Rodney the Giant?" "That's right, it's me, Rodney the Giant!" "Doug The Crow came to me and told me that you guys were causing him and Carey the Dragon trouble, so we made a deal!" "I'm going to take you back to my castle and eat you all for lunch!" Detective Jon yelled to everyone, "what are we going to do?"

Chapter 7
Escaping Rodney
The Giants
Castle

Rodney the Giant took them back to his castle and put them in a cage! While he was getting the stove ready to cook them and eat them for lunch, Detective Jon told everyone, "we have to get out of here!" Ralph the Wizard and the others we're like, "but how?" Detective Jon had an idea. He had a paperclip in his pocket. "If I can pick the lock of the cage, perhaps we can quickly escape!"

He got up on Bentley the Trolls back and tried to pick the lock. Success ! He eventually got the door of the cage open and they started to escape really quietly! However Rodney the Giant spotted them! Everyone screamed "run!" they were all running down the castle hallways with Rodney the Giant chasing them! They were running as fast as they could, all across the castle! Suddenly, they came to a dead end! Everyone was like, "what do we do now Detective Jon?" The Oatmeal Warlock had an idea! He said to Detective Jon, "quick, use the ice element towards the giant!" Detective Jon released the power of the ice element towards Rodney the Giant! Rodney the Giant was like, "oh no!" The ice element froze the giant until he was completely frozen solid! Everyone was like, "hooray for Detective Jon!" Quickly everyone scurried out the castle window on their way to Carey the Dragon's cave. Meanwhile Doug The Crow finally delivered Ralph the Wizard's wand to Carey the Dragon! She was like, "this is perfect!" "There is nothing that can stop me now from taking over the universe!" "I will now open the portal to earth and destroy it!" Meanwhile back at the museum on earth, Megan the Museum Manager and Sally were in the museum garden having a nice cup of tea and wondering how Detective Jon was doing. Sally was like, "I hope he's okay!" Just then they noticed that a huge portal had opened up in the sky! Both Megan the Museum manager and Sally agreed, "That Can't be good!"

Chapter 8
Entering Carey
The Dragon's
Cave

Detective Jon and everyone on the hidden world arrived At Carey The Dragon's Cave which was surrounded by lava. Suddenly they noticed a portal up in the sky had been opened! Ralph the Wizard said, "we must hurry before Carey the Dragon and Doug The Crow head to your world!" Detective Jon had an idea, "we will use the ice element to freeze the lava!" So Detective Jon used the ice element to freeze the lava, and they crossed over to the cave. Then they headed into the cave where they saw none other than Carey the Dragon herself and her crow Doug! She said "you must be DetectiveJon?" "Well, you're too late!" "I have already opened the portal to your world Detective Jon, and there's nothing you can do to stop me now!" "First I will destroy your world and then the universe!" Detective Jon said, "you won't get away with this!" Carey the Dragon and Doug the Crow said, "we will!" and then they both flew into the portal! Detective Jon was wondering how he was going to get up high enough to reach the portal? He grabbed all 3 elements from his pocket and all of a sudden they started floating around him! They all came together and Detective Jon became Super Detective Jon! Everyone was astonished! Wow!! Super Detective Jon started flying up to the portal, heading back to his world. Everyone was like, "don't worry Super Detective Jon, we will catch up!" So Super Detective Jon was on his way back to his world to stop Carey the Dragon and Doug the Crow once and for all!

Chapter 9
The Final Battle

Megan the museum manager, and Sally we're still wondering what was going on with the sky! All of a sudden they saw a crow come out of the portal! Then they saw something big and green come out of the portal! Megan the Museum manager said, "is that a dragon?" And then, all of a sudden, Sally said "look!" It was Detective Jon, but he looked different! Carey the Dragon started using her fire breath to destroy the museum! Everyone was panicking and trying to escape to their cars! But Doug the Crow used Ralph the Wizard's magic wand to destroy their cars! Everyone was panicking and screaming, "run, it's the end of the world!" Just then Super Detective Jon appeared and told everyone "everything's going to be fine!" Doug the Crow saw Detective Jon had his new superpowers and he said, "oh no, he's got the power of the elements!" "I must destroy him now!" So Doug The Crow used Ralph the Wizard's magic wand and aimed it right at Super Detective Jon! Sally screamed, "lookout Super Detective Jon!" Super Detective Jon quickly used his ice element powers to freeze Doug The Crow! He then picked up Ralph the Wizard's magic wand! Then Carey the Dragon saw that Super Detective Jon had the magic wand that she had stolen from Ralph the Wizard! "I must destroy him at all costs!" So she started using her fire breath at Super Detective Jon! Super Detective Jon quickly started using the fire element back at Carey the Dragon! She yelled, "that hurt!" Then Super DetectiveJon used the water element powers to fight against Carey the Dragon's fire breath! Eventually she was all out of breath! But Carey the Dragon said, "I can still squash you with my tail!" So she tried desperately to squash him! However Super Detective Jon used Ralph the Wizard's magic wand to open another portal and then quickly used the power of the fire element to push Carey the Dragon Into the portal! He then threw frozen Doug the Crow in with her! Carey the Dragon screamed, "no It can't be!" "It can't be!" Defeated, Carey the Dragon lost her grip, and both were sucked into the portal, and the portal closed! Everyone was cheering for Super Detective Jon! However, Super Detective Jon's powers disappeared! Shortly Megan the Museum Manager said, "look the portal is still open in the sky!" Suddenly, Ralph the Wizard, Sophia the Unicorn, Bentley the Troll and the Oatmeal Warlock all came out of the portal! They had some unfortunate news!

Chapter 10
Goodbye Detective Jon

Ralph the Wizard said to Detective Jon, "In order for the portal to close, it must be closed from the hidden world." Detective Jon said to Ralph the Wizard, "okay, here is your wand back." Ralph the Wizard said, "I'm afraid you don't understand, in order for the portal to close, you have to do it!" Then Detective Jon realized what he had to do! "You mean I have to go back to the Hidden World with you,and I can't come back to my world?" Ralph the Wizard said "I'm afraid so, now that you've taken possession of the wand, you are now the wand's owner, and only you have the power to close the portal!" "You have to go back to the Hidden World to close the portal!" Detective Jon was like, "no, there must be some other way?" "I'm afraid there isn't," said Ralph the Wizard. Megan the Museum Manager and sally we're upset and crying, saying, there must be another way?" Ralph the Wizard again said, I'm afraid there isn't!" "If the portal was going to remain open I'm afraid both worlds would be eventually swallowed up!" Detective Jon finally agreed that It had to be done to save the universe, and said to Megan the Museum Manager and Sally, "I'm going to miss you both!" "I can't thank both of you enough for all the support you've given me!" Everyone there was also crying and waving goodbye to Detective Jon as he headed towards the portal. Suddenly, he was gone! Detective Jon and Ralph the Wizard, along with everyone else from the Hidden World made it back! Ralph the Wizard said, "are you ready for this Detective Jon?" And he said," I'm ready!" So he used the magic wand one more time to close the portal for good! He had said goodbye to his friends on the other side of the portal forever! The worlds were saved once again! Now everyone in Detective Jon's world could not believe that he was gone!

Megan the museum manager finally finished rebuilding her museum after Carey the Dragon had destroyed it, and was wondering if Detective Jon would be okay living in the Hidden World. Sally came up to Megan the Museum Manager and said, "I'm sure he's going to be just fine!" "I'm throwing a party at my mansion, would you like to come?" Megan the Museum Manager said "sure!" So, what did happen to Detective Jon? Well, he started taking magic lessons from Ralph the Wizard on how to use his magic wand! He was doing a great job, and he was Ralph the Wizard's number one student! Meanwhile Sally and Megan the Museum Manager became very close friends, and they all lived happily ever after!

THE END

About the Author

Isaiah who has autism resides in the beautiful Okanagan Valley which is situated in the Southern part of British Columbia, Canada. Taking in the latest movies at the local theaters is one of his favorite pass times. His interest in solving mysteries has lead to his desire to write about them. His books is full of exciting plots and adventures. Playing video games keeps him busy the majority of his time but finds time in his sometimes hectic schedule to write and looks forward to publishing more of his work.

www.ingramcontent.com/pod-product-compliance
Lightning Source LLC
Chambersburg PA
CBHW052234150726
48002CB00003B/1418